BABY
ELEPHANT

A Grosset & Dunlap **ALL ABOARD BOOK**®

There are two kinds of elephants:
African elephants and Asian elephants.
This book is about a baby African elephant.

Text copyright © 1997 by Lucille Recht Penner. Illustrations copyright © 1997 by Betina Ogden. All rights reserved. Published by Grosset & Dunlap, Inc., a member of The Putnam & Grosset Group, New York. GROSSET & DUNLAP is a trademark of Grosset & Dunlap, Inc. ALL ABOARD BOOKS is a trademark of Grosset & Dunlap, Inc. Registered in U.S. Patent and Trademark Office. THE LITTLE ENGINE THAT COULD and engine design are trademarks of Platt & Munk, Publishers, which is a division of Grosset & Dunlap, Inc. Published simultaneously in Canada. Printed in the U.S.A.

Library of Congress Cataloging-in-Publication Data

Penner, Lucille Recht.
  Baby elephant / by Lucille Recht Penner ; illustrated by Betina Ogden.
    p.   cm. — (All aboard books)
  Summary: Describes the physical characteristics and behavior of a herd of African elephants and the day in the life of a new baby born among them.
    1. African elephant—Infancy—Juvenile literature.   2. African elephant—Behavior—Juvenile literature.
3. Parental behavior in animals—Juvenile literature.   [1. African elephant.   2. Elephants.]   I. Ogden, Betina, ill.   II. Title.   III. Series: Grosset & Dunlap all aboard book.
  QL737.P98P395   1997
  599.67'4139—dc21

                                                                                96-37396
                                                                                CIP
                                                                                AC

ISBN 0-448-41497-X   A B C D E F G H I J

BABY ELEPHANT

By Lucille Recht Penner

Illustrated by Betina Ogden

Grosset & Dunlap, Publishers

On the plains of eastern Africa, a little gray elephant is born. He staggers to his feet. His eyes are red, his head is covered with soft, reddish hair, and his ears are bright pink. He takes a few wobbly steps, trips over his trunk, and sprawls on the ground.

Gently, his huge mother pulls him up with her trunk and front foot.

Other elephants come running. They are the baby's sisters, aunts, and cousins. The biggest elephant is the baby's grandmother. She is almost sixty years old and is the leader of the group.

The elephants sniff the baby, touch him with their trunks, and rumble softly to welcome him to the family.

An elephant family is made up of adult females and their children. The young elephants are called calves. There are about twelve elephants in a family. They eat, sleep, and play together. Many families sometimes travel together in a huge herd.

Where is the baby's father? Like most adult male elephants, he lives by himself or with a small group of other males. When the baby is about fourteen years old, he will go off to live on his own, too.

A tall giraffe comes out of the trees. He is curious about the new baby, but the mother elephant won't let him come near. She shakes her head. Her ears make a sharp sound. *Crack!* It's a warning. *Stay away from my baby!*

The baby elephant squeals. He is hungry! His mother answers with a soft, humming sound. Then she helps him stand between her front legs to nurse.

The little elephant reaches only halfway up his mother's leg, but he already weighs more than most full-grown men. He curls his trunk over his head and sucks up his first meal of sweet milk.

The grandmother elephant gives a low, rumbling call, and the other elephants fall into line behind her. She will lead them to the best places to find food and water.

Elephants are very intelligent. They are good at learning and remembering. In some parts of Africa, elephants still walk on paths that were made long ago by their great-great-grandparents.

The new baby walks close beside his mother. He is safe there. She touches him often with her trunk. If he trips and falls, she helps him up and they go on. The whole family walks slowly to make it easy for the baby to keep up.

The baby's older sister walks behind her mother. Sometimes she holds on to her tail with her trunk.

In the forest, the elephants spread out and begin to eat. They call to each other often so that no one gets lost.

Some of the elephants are eating bark. They tear off long strips with their trunks. Others use their tusks to dig up roots.

Tusks are long, pointed, ivory teeth. For many years, hunters have killed elephants for their beautiful ivory tusks. Today, Kenya, Zaire, and other African countries where many elephants live have laws to protect the elephants from ivory hunters.

The baby elephant has little baby tusks. When he is about two years old, they will fall out and his new tusks will come in. They may grow to be eight feet long!

An adult elephant eats about 350 pounds of food a day! Elephants need this much food because they are so big. They are the biggest animals in the world, except for whales. The baby's grandmother is almost ten feet tall and weighs one thousand pounds!

Elephants are also very strong. *Smash!* Some elephants ram trees with their heads. They knock them down and eat the tender green leaves on the top branches.

The baby's mother uses her trunk and huge feet to help get food. First she wraps her trunk around a clump of grass and pulls it tight. Then she kicks it. Her strong toenails break right through the grass.

The baby elephant doesn't know how to use his trunk to pick up food. Instead, he stretches it out to touch and sniff things. Elephants have an amazing sense of smell. They can smell water five miles away!

The baby plays with his trunk, swinging it in a circle. Sometimes he gets it into his mouth and sucks it until it falls out again.

An elephant's trunk is really its nose and upper lip. The two small bumps at the tip are used just the way we use our fingers. These elephant "fingers" can pick up a berry or a single blade of grass.

At noon the sun is very hot. The elephant family takes a nap under a clump of tall trees. The adults nap standing up. Some rest their trunks on their tusks. Only their big ears move, flapping back and forth to cool them off.

The baby elephant flops down in the shade
between his mother's legs and falls fast asleep.
She rests her trunk next to his head.

When they wake up, the elephants are thirsty. They go to the river to drink. A herd of zebras are already drinking, but they move away to make room for the elephants.

The baby's mother sucks up a trunkful of water and squirts it into her mouth. *Aaaaaah!*

Splash! Some of the elephants plunge into the river to swim. Elephants can swim underwater. They hold up the tips of their trunks to breathe.

The mother elephant gives her baby a shower. It feels *good!*

Near the riverbank are pools of thick red mud. Elephants love mud! It feels cool and it's good protection for their skin. An elephant has thick, wrinkly skin, but it is still tender. An insect bite hurts and so does a sunburn. A coat of gooey mud is good protection.

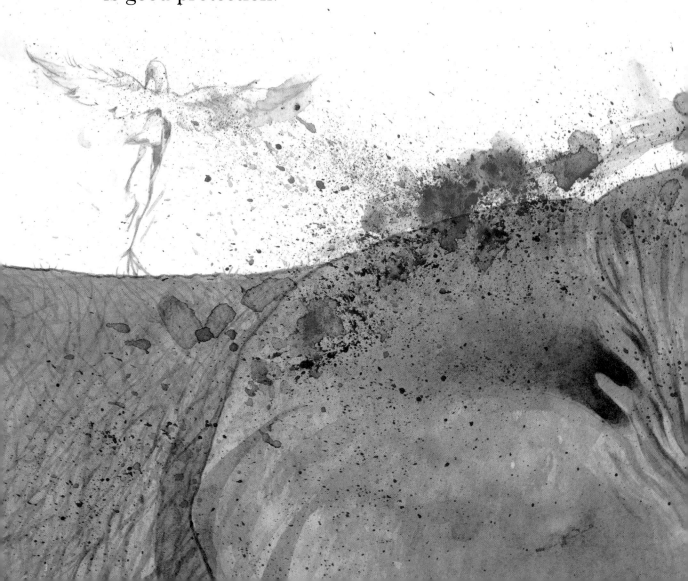

The adults use their trunks to splash mud over themselves, but the calves just jump in and wiggle around. Soon they are the dark red color of the mud.

After their mud bath, the calves play. Some chase each other in circles, squealing and grunting. One runs after a friendly baboon.

Another finds a stick and tosses it in the air.

This little elephant is climbing on his big sister. It is another way elephants play.

As the wind blows through the trees, the grandmother raises her trunk and sniffs the air. The other elephants lift their trunks, too. They smell a lion!

Quickly, the biggest elephants form a tight circle around the calves. They stretch out their great ears, which makes them look enormous. Some of them trumpet and stamp the ground, throwing up clouds of dust. If the lion comes close, they will charge.

But the lion is afraid. He runs away. The elephants are safe.

Now the baby elephant's day is almost over. In the fading light, the family gathers together. One by one, the little calves sink to the ground.

As the stars grow bright, the baby closes his eyes. All around him, the breathing of his family makes a sound like the wind.